IGGY THE URK:
EUUUGH!
EYEBALL
STEW!

Alan MacDonald

Illustrated by Mark Beech

First published in 2011
by Bloomsbury Publishing plc
This Large Print edition published by
AudioGO Ltd 2012
by arrangement with
Bloomsbury Publishing plc

ISBN: 978 1445 823560

British Library Cataloguing in Publication Data available

Printed and bound in Great Britain by
MPG Books Group Limited

Contents

Long, long ago . . .

Really ages ago. The world was a wild and barren place. There were no houses or shops, no schools or teachers, no cars, flushing toilets or peanut-butter sandwiches. So many things didn't exist that to write them all down would fill every page of this book and leave no room for the story.

If you want to imagine how the world was, imagine an endless landscape of mountains, forests, rocks and stones. In fact, stones lay everywhere, because this was . . .

THE STONE AGE

In the forests lived savage beasts—bears, snaggle-toothed tigers and woolly mammoths, which looked like elephants badly in need of a haircut. People generally avoided the forests. They lived together in tribes because it was safer that way and easier on the cooking. One such tribe was the Urks.

The Urks were a warlike race with bushy beards and hairy legs—especially some of the women. Their clothes were made of animal skins and they lived in caves high on a hill, overlooking the Valley of Urk and the river winding through it. In one of these caves lived a boy called Iggy. He wasn't the tallest or the hairiest in his tribe, but what he did have was imagination, and this got him into a whole heap of trouble. That of course is another story . . . Luckily it's the story that's about to begin . . .

Chapter 1

Never Look a Rhino in the Eye

Something was definitely happening. All over the hill the Urks were emerging from their caves and hurrying down the slope towards the forest. Iggy caught sight of his best friend, Hubba, among the crowd.

'What's going on?' he called.

'Rhino!' shouted Hubba excitedly. 'Snark's seen tracks in the forest!'

Iggy didn't need to hear any more; he plunged back into the cave to collect his weapons. If there was going to be a rhino hunt, he didn't want to miss it. He had never actually seen a woolly rhinoceros, though of course he knew all about them. He knew they were fearsome beasts with sharp horns and tempers shorter than Hubba's legs. He knew too that if an angry rhino charged you had better not get in its way.

4

It was typical that it was Snark who'd spotted the tracks. Snark never tired of telling Iggy that (in his opinion) he was the best hunter in the tribe. But this was Iggy's chance to prove him wrong. He had something that Snark didn't. Slung over his shoulder, he carried the long curved stick that was his latest invention. So far there hadn't been a real chance to try it out, but he was pretty certain it would prove deadly.

When he caught up with the rest of the hunting party they were moving swiftly and silently through the forest. All the best hunters in the tribe were there including Iggy's dad, Snark, Borg and even Hammerhead himself. The grizzled old chief rarely hunted these days but even he couldn't resist the prospect of tracking a woolly rhino.

'Where's your spear?' whispered Dad.

'Oh, I left it at home. I've got this,' said Iggy, unhooking the stick from his shoulder.

'What the Urk's that?'

'A boo, I made it. It makes a kind of *boo!* noise when you shoot these arrow

5

things.'

He handed his dad one of the flint-tipped arrows he'd spent hours making. Dad grunted.

'What's wrong with a spear?'

'Nothing, but these are better,' said Iggy. 'I've been practising. I can hit a tree nine times out of ten.'

'We're not hunting trees, boy.'

'I know, but this will work. I know it will.'

'Humph!' said Dad. 'Just don't go pointing her at anyone.' He walked away, shaking his head and muttering under his breath.

Iggy sighed. His last idea had been the jawbone clatterpult—which even he had to admit was not a total success. It was brilliant if you were hunting, say, a toad or a lizard, but not much use if you were faced with a stampeding

mammoth. Nevertheless it had given him the idea for something better. If you could shoot stones, he reasoned, then why not other things like little spears? It had taken weeks of work and patience but finally he had perfected the boo and arrow. He tested the boo string for the hundredth time. It was made from animal gut and made a satisfying *twang* when you let it go. He imagined taking aim at a huge woolly rhino as it came bursting through the trees. Maybe today would be the day?

Hammerhead and the others were squatting down, studying something in the mud.

'Fresh tracks. It come this way,' said Dad, tracing the outline of some large footprints.

'Rhino?' asked Hammerhead.

'Well, it's not a rabbit. What you want us to do, Chief?'

Hammerhead scratched his beard. The truth was he didn't really have any kind of plan. He was hoping they would run into the rhino and kill it, preferably without having to get too close.

'We're wasting us time, we should

drive her to the Crags,' said Borg impatiently.

Hammerhead stood up and gave him an icy stare.

'Where's your whalebone necklace?' he asked.

'Uh? I doesn't have one,' replied Borg.

'But I has; that's why I'm Chief,' said Hammerhead. 'We do as I say, right?'

Borg nodded sulkily.

'So what are we doing, Chief?' repeated Iggy's dad.

Hammerhead considered, glancing up at the grey sky.

'We'll drive her to the Crags.'

*   *   *

Mammoth Crags lay beyond the forest—a tall dome of brown rock rising above a valley. It was a favourite hunting ploy of the Urks to climb the Crags and lie in wait. When the rhino passed by they would launch their attack, raining down rocks and spears from above. It was simple but effective, with the added advantage that no one got killed (apart from the rhino). The only downside of the plan was that someone had to drive the beast out of the forest and towards the Crags. Iggy wondered which poor fool the Chief was going to pick.

*   *   *

One hour later he was tramping through the forest, beating the undergrowth with a stick. His arm ached and he was sweating. So far the only beast he and Hubba had flushed out was a startled frog. Iggy had come on the hunt hoping to impress everyone with his new invention, but this way they wouldn't even take part in the kill. He waded through cold muddy water, cutting with his stick at a clump of tall reeds. Suddenly he was startled by something that leapt out. He caught a glimpse of red hair and wide, frightened eyes. A girl. The next moment she was off, scrabbling up the bank and crashing through the trees.

'HEY, WAIT!' yelled Iggy. He signalled to Hubba and the two of them gave chase.

They plunged through the forest, dropping their sticks and weaving through the trees. Iggy forgot all about the woolly rhino—all he could think about was catching up with the girl. He lost sight of her, then saw a flash of red hair up ahead.

Finally they emerged from the trees and stood panting for breath. They had reached the dusty valley where the river had dried up. Just ahead were Mammoth Crags, the dark rocks rising to a dizzy height. Iggy could see the hunting party crouched on top, making a hopeless attempt to keep out of sight. Just short of the Crags he caught sight of the red-haired girl. She was standing perfectly still, gazing at something to her left. Iggy turned his head and saw it: a huge male rhino, shaggy and brown, moody as an ogre with toothache. The girl gazed spellbound at the rhino and it looked right back. Iggy tried to remember what you should do in this kind of situation. He was pretty sure it wasn't challenge the rhino to a staring match.

WOOLLY RHINOCEROS

Size: Huge. Up to 3.5 metres long

Weight: 4 tonnes (as heavy as 50 Urks)

Diet: Mosses, herbs, low-growing plants

Features: Long fur, thick legs, short temper

Weapons: Pair of wickedly sharp horns

Speed: Up to 30 miles an hour on the charge

Things NOT TO do if a rhino charges:

a) Turn your back
b) Do your hilarious rhino impression
c) Shout 'Hey, big nose! Can't catch me!'

*   *   *

The rhinoceros tossed back its head and stirred the dust with one of its massive feet.

'It's going to charge,' whispered Hubba.

Iggy nodded. 'Why doesn't she run?'

'Maybe she's too tired.'

Iggy couldn't bear to watch any longer.

'RUN!' he shouted. *'RUN!'*

The red-haired girl didn't seem to hear— either that or she was frozen with terror. Iggy quickly unhooked the boo from his shoulder and took aim with one of his arrows. He hesitated. The rhino's hide was tough as armour. One arrow might not be enough to bring it down and there would be no time to shoot a second. He couldn't risk it. There was only one chance and that was to reach the girl before it was too late.

The rhino lowered its head, snorted and lumbered forward. Iggy didn't stop to think. He set off, running fast across the stony ground.

'Iggy, no!' cried Hubba.

The girl turned her head towards him, her eyes wide and frightened. The ground shook like an earth tremor as the rhino gained speed, pounding towards her. The curved horn on its snout was aimed at her ribs, ready to toss her high into the air. Iggy didn't know if he would make it. At the last moment he threw himself through the air on top of the girl. They hit the ground with a thud. A second later the rhino thundered past in a storm of dust, so close that Iggy could have counted its horny toenails.

He sat up and looked around, still

shaking. The red-haired girl coughed and spat out a mouthful of dirt. Luckily for them woolly rhinos have short memories and brains the size of a sultana. This one had already forgotten them and was chewing on a straggly plant underneath the brown cliffs.

'NOW!' yelled a voice. Iggy looked up in time to see a giant boulder come hurtling down.

KADUUUUUUNK!

It landed just short of the rhino, shattering into a million pieces. The creature turned its head and grunted

14

as if this kind of thing happened all the time. It ambled lazily back towards the forest.

Iggy looked up at the faces peering over the rocks.

'Huh!' said Hammerhead. 'Told you it'd never work!'

Chapter 2

Firestones are For Ever

Mum was not impressed. She was expecting some nice rhino meat for supper, but instead Iggy had returned with an extra mouth to feed. He could tell she was annoyed by the way she kept stabbing at the fire with a stick.

'Who is she?' she scowled.

'I'm not sure,' replied Iggy. 'Her name's Oosha. She almost got trampled by a woolly rhino. I think she's a bit upset.'

'Upset? I'll give her upset!' snapped Mum, brandishing her stick. 'What am I meant to feed her? And where's she gonna sleep, I'd like to know?'

'Well . . . with us,' said Iggy.

'Talk sense, boy! There's no room.'

True the cave had got a bit cluttered lately, what with all the sticks, feathers and flints that Iggy needed for making arrows. But he could tidy up, or at least shove all the mess to the back.

'She could be anyone! A savage!' grumbled Mum. 'What if we wake up an' find we're all dead?'

'We won't!' sighed Iggy. 'Anyway, if you're dead you won't wake up.'

He broke off. Oosha had come out of the cave, where she had been trying to get some rest. She was about Iggy's age with bright red hair woven into braids. Most of the girls Iggy knew had hair the colour of mud (apart from Umily, the Chief's daughter).

Oosha went over to Iggy's mum and reached out a hand, touching her cheek.

'Putty,' she said.

'Uhh?' frowned Mum. 'Who's she calling potty?'

'Pretty,' said Iggy. 'She said you're pretty.'

'Don't talk soft.' Mum went back to stabbing the fire but Iggy could tell she was pleased.

After supper they made up a bed of furs for their visitor near the back of the cave. Mum kept a hunting axe beside her during the night—just in case.

*   *   *

Next morning when Iggy woke up the girl had gone. Her furs lay neatly folded in a pile. He found her outside the cave where she already had a fire going. It seemed like a good chance to try and find out a bit more about her.

'I'm Iggy,' he began. 'We are Urks.'

Oosha looked puzzled.

'This is our home—the Valley of Urk.' He pointed to the hillside with its rocks and caves. Oosha laughed. She probably hadn't the faintest idea what he was talking about. He tried again.

'Where do you come from?' he asked. 'WHERE—OOSHA—FROM?'

Oosha pointed at him. 'Iggy!'

'Yes, I'm Iggy . . .'

'Iggy brave!'

'Yes . . .'

'Save Oosha life!'

'I know,' said Iggy. 'But what about you? WHERE IS YOUR HOME? HOME?' He pointed to his cave. Oosha seemed to grasp his meaning.

She dragged him to the edge of the hill and pointed beyond the forest to a range of blue-grey mountains in the distance.

'That's where you live—the Cloud Mountains?'

Oosha nodded.

'But who are your tribe?'

'Henna!'

Henna. Iggy had never heard of such a tribe, but then again he'd never been as far as the Cloud Mountains. He had only seen them on a clear day when there was a break in the rain or fog.

'My father mighty big cheat,' said Oosha.

'Cheat?'

'Yes. Big Cheat of Henna!'

'I think she means Big Chief.' Iggy turned to see that his dad was awake and had been listening to their conversation. At least they were starting to get somewhere. If Oosha was a chief's daughter, then she must be important. People would be looking for her. But what was she doing wandering around in the forest getting herself chased by woolly rhinos? Iggy tried another question.

'How did you find us?'

'Oosha lost.'

'You lost your tribe?'

Oosha nodded. 'I scare. Then I see hairy nossrus. I scare to sick.'

'And that were when Iggy saved you?' said Dad.

Oosha looked at Iggy with shining eyes. 'Iggy brave. Brave worrier.'

Iggy went a little pink. He'd been called a lot of things, but never a brave worrier before. Not even by Umily when he had rescued her from the terrible Slimosaur.

Oosha was taking off one of the long necklaces she wore. She held it out

to him. It had a single crimson stone which sparkled like morning frost. Iggy had never seen anything so beautiful in all his life.

'For you, Iggy,' said Oosha. 'Oosha make thank.'

'It's amazing,' said Iggy. 'What is it?'

'Firestone,' answered Oosha. 'She bring you good luck.'

*   *   *

Iggy wore the red firestone proudly round his neck, over the wolf-fang necklace that he'd been given when he became a Son of Urk. It drew admiring looks from the rest of the tribe.

Yet over the next few days he was dissappointed to find that he wasn't the only person to own one of the beautiful stones. Oosha seemed to give them away freely to anyone she met. Other members of the tribe took to wearing firestones on bracelets, necklaces, or even dangling from their ears. Hammerhead was overheard talking to his daughter about the red stones and wondering if someone might want to make him a gift of one.

Normally the Urks were suspicious of outsiders, but as the days turned to weeks, they grew used to Oosha's presence and even began to accept her. They liked her friendly smile and the funny way she talked. The women sat happily while she braided their hair or combed it with an old fishbone. The men liked the way she listened to their hunting stories, gasping when they described how they'd overcome a woolly mammoth by tying its trunk in knots. Not everyone was impressed with the newcomer, however, as Iggy found out when he bumped into Umily, the Chief's daughter. The two of them had become close friends after the adventure with the Slimosaur, but since Oosha's arrival Iggy had seen little of Umily.

'Huh! You as well,' Umily grunted, pointing to the stone round his neck.

Iggy touched it. 'Oosha gave it to me. Isn't it beautiful?'

Umily shrugged. She didn't seem that impressed.

'Oosha says her people call them firestones,' explained Iggy.

'Good for Oosha,' said Umily. She walked faster, heading up the hill towards her cave. Iggy tried to keep up with her.

'Why don't you like her?' he asked.

'Who said I doesn't?'

'It's pretty obvious. You've hardly spoken to her.'

'So? What's it to you?'

'I just want to know, that's all.'

Umily sighed wearily and turned to face him.

'All right, tell me one thing,' she said. 'What's she want?'

Iggy looked puzzled. He spread his hands. 'Nothing!'

'No?' said Umily. 'All them firestones she gives away. Why? What's she after?'

Iggy stared. He couldn't believe Umily could be so suspicious. 'Maybe she's grateful I saved her life,' he said. 'Maybe she's the kind of person who likes giving presents.'

Umily snorted.

'Anyway,' said Iggy, ' I don't see why you're so cross.'

'CROSS?' said Umily, turning on him. 'I'M NOT CROSS! I COULDN'T CARE LESS!'

She stomped off up the hill as if the grass needed flattening. Iggy stared after her with his mouth open.

Chapter 3

Flinted

The following evening Iggy found Oosha sitting on a rock above the valley, watching the sun sink slowly in the west. At supper she'd been quieter than usual and didn't want any wild pig's liver. In fact Iggy had never seen her taste meat at all.

He sat down beside her. Her eyes searched out the mountains in the far distance which were streaked with red.

'I expect you miss it,' said Iggy.

'Missit?'

'Your home.'

Oosha shook her head. 'I happy here. Like cave. Like Valley. Like making frogs.'

'Making friends,' said Iggy. After two weeks Oosha's Urkish was improving but she still got certain words muddled. They watched the setting sun for a while.

'But still, you must want to go home,' said Iggy.

Oosha shook her head. 'Home far. Many walk.'

'But you know the way?'

'Forest not safe like cave,' said Oosha. 'Full of animal—boors and welves.'

Iggy knew what she meant. His mum and dad were always warning him not to go to the forest by himself. By day it was a dangerous place and at night it was downright scary. Besides, Oosha was a girl—she probably didn't know how to handle an axe or shoot a boo and arrow. If she was ever going to get home, she'd need help—someone strong and brave to protect her.

'Why don't I come with you?' said Iggy. 'I could look out for bears and wolves. Make sure you get home safely.'

Oosha looked alarmed. 'No, Iggy. I not ask this.'

'Why not? You can't stay for ever. What about your father, the Big Cheat? He'll be worried about you.'

'Mmm,' said Oosha. 'But you have

Cheat. Hogglehead. He not let me go back.'

Iggy shrugged. 'I don't see why he'd stop us. He's my uncle so I'll talk to him if you like.'

Oosha nodded doubtfully. Talking about going home seemed to make her worried. Iggy supposed it was natural. She must be homesick. She probably didn't want to get her hopes up in case it didn't happen. In any case, he thought, it wasn't a bad idea to get Hammerhead's permission. If the High Chief agreed to the trip, then his parents could hardly refuse.

*   *   *

In a large cave further up the hill, Hammerhead and Borg sat opposite each other absorbed in a game of Flints. Like most games the Urks enjoyed, it had very simple rules.

HOW TO PLAY FLINTS
1. *There are two players. Each starts with a small pile of flints.*
2. *The object of the game is to win your*

opponent's flints until he is 'flinted' (or out).
3. *The player who starts holds out his fist in front of him. His opponent must try to guess how many flints he is holding.*
4. *If a player guesses correctly he gains the flints for his own pile. If he is wrong his opponent whacks him hard on the knuckles. (This is called 'knuckling'.)*
5. *Players are allowed to put each other off by humming, farting, pulling faces or choosing a difficult number like five.*

Hammerhead was usually clueless at Flints, but today he seemed to be on a winning streak. Beside him was a large pile of shiny black stones, while Borg was down to his last three. It was the Chief's turn to guess. Borg brought his fist out in front of him and recited the traditional rhyme:

> '*Mud in your eye, mud in your ear,*
> *How many flints do I got here?*'

The Chief stared at Borg's fist, trying to decide. His opponent had only three flints left, which, according to the Chief's calculations, meant he must be holding one, two or all three of his flints (unless it was none). So far Hammerhead's guesses had proved uncannily accurate, almost as if Borg was letting him win. He made up his mind.

'One!' he said. 'No, wait . . . Two!'

Borg raised his eyebrows.

'Three!' cried Hammerhead. 'You got three!'

'Is that your guess?'

'Yes, three.'

Borg groaned. He opened his hand to reveal three small black flints.

'HA! I winned again!' bellowed

29

Hammerhead in triumph. He collected his winnings and added them to the large pile of flints beside him. 'One more round?' he suggested.

Borg turned up the palms of his hands. 'How? I'm flinted.'

'Come on! You must have more!'

Borg shook his head. 'That were the last. Unless . . .'

'What?'

'Unless you want to raise the stakes, like?'

Borg reached inside his furs and brought something out. The Chief's eyes lit up. It was a firestone the size of a ripe plum. In the dim light of the cave it seemed to glow and wink like a diamond. Hammerhead had seen his nephew, Iggy, wearing a stone like this and ever since he had been dying to get his hands on one. It was just the kind of thing a ruggedly handsome Chief ought to wear.

'So, one more game?' asked Borg.

'Let's play.'

Borg laughed softly. 'And what's in it for me?'

'Flints.   I   got   plenty,' said

Hammerhead, indicating his pile.

Borg shook his head. 'Flints I can get. This is worth a thousand. Look at her!'

Hammerhead was looking—in fact he was having trouble tearing his eyes away. Borg turned the crimson stone so that tiny pinpricks of light raced across the roof of the cave. It was hypnotic.

'What do you want for her?' asked Hammerhead, wiping the dribble from his beard.

'Depends what you got.'

Hammerhead cast around his cave. 'Skins? Furs? Mammoth horns? Name your price.'

Borg's eyes narrowed to slits. There was only one thing he wanted and it was hanging round his opponent's neck: the ceremonial whalebone necklace passed down from one High Chief to the next. Just as a king needs a crown, no chief could rule the tribe without the necklace.

'One more game,' said Borg. 'But let's make it interesting . . .'

'HELLO?'

Borg cursed his luck. Someone had

31

blundered in, just when he was getting so close! Why didn't people learn to knock at a cave before entering? Quickly he tucked the firestone inside his furs, out of sight. His business with Hammerhead would have to wait for another day.

'Oh, sorry, Chief,' said Iggy, coming in. 'I didn't know you were in the middle of a game.'

'That's all right,' said Hammerhead. 'Borg were just going. He's flinted. So what brings you here?'

Iggy took a deep breath. He wished Borg would hurry up and go—the grim-faced elder gave him the creeps.

'It's about Oosha,' he said.

'Who?'

'You know, the girl we found in the forest. She's been staying with us but I think she wants to go home.'

'Ah.' Hammerhead looked relieved. He thought it might be some difficult question like what to do about the dreadful stink from the bone-pit. 'What's it to do with me?' he asked.

'Well, you're Chief,' Iggy reminded him.

'High Chief.'

'Yes, High Chief. So I thought we should ask your permission.'

'Permission? Oh well—hmm—that's different!' said Hammerhead. 'I got to think about that.'

He stood up and put on his deep thinking expression, which was very similar to his I've-eaten-too-many-nuts expression. He paced up and down a few times, then looked up.

'I've decided. She can go.'

Borg coughed loudly. 'Is that wise? This Henna girl, what do we know about her?'

'Not much,' admitted Hammerhead. 'I didn't even know she were a girl.'

'Just my point. Then how do we know she's not . . . a SPY?'

Hammerhead looked startled. 'What do you mean?'

33

'Maybe her tribe sent her,' Borg went on. 'Maybe they're out to steal our caves, or our women.'

'Or our flints!' cried Hammerhead.

'But Chief, she's not a spy!' protested Iggy. 'All she wants is to go home. What if I go with her?'

'Hmm, I don't know,' said Hammerhead. 'It's a risk.'

Iggy's eye fell on the shining pile of flints on the ground. 'Oh,' he said. 'Did I mention her father is a Chief?'

Hammerhead looked up. 'No!'

'Obviously not a High Chief, but still, I'm sure he'd be grateful if we return his missing daughter. He might even offer some sort of *reward*.'

'Reward? Like what?' said Hammerhead.

'I don't know,' said Iggy. 'Maybe some of these stones. He touched the gleaming firestone hanging round his neck.

Borg saw the look of pure greed in Hammerhead's eyes. It was remarkable the attraction of these little stones, he thought. They cast a spell over people. If he could just get his hands on a

34

dozen or more, what power he would have then! He would make a necklace that would drive someone mad with desire—someone like Hammerhead, for instance. The old fool would give anything to possess them. But first things first. He needed the firestones— and the girl could lead him to them.

'Maybe the boy's right,' he said. 'If she's a Chief's daughter, we should help her get home.'

'Really?' said Iggy, surprised to find Borg agreeing with him.

'Certainly,' nodded Hammerhead. 'It's our duty. And if there's a reward ...'

'I only said there *might* be,' said Iggy.

'But if there is, then I should claim it—as Chief, like.'

'Just one thing,' said Borg. 'This tribe—the Henna. Where do they live?'

'In the Cloud Mountains,' replied Iggy.

'A long way. We can't have you

going by yourself.'

'I thought of that,' said Iggy. 'That's why I'm taking Hubba.'

Borg laughed drily. 'Even so. Take someone else—someone who can hunt.'

'Makes sense,' agreed Hammerhead. 'Who was you thinking?'

Borg stroked his chin, pretending to consider the question. His face brightened.

'I know,' he said. 'What about Snark?'

Chapter 4

And Snark Makes Three

'SNARK?' groaned Hubba, when he heard the news. 'What's he coming for?'

'Don't blame me!' said Iggy. 'It wasn't my idea. His dad insisted.'

'Yes, but why Snark?'

'Who is Snork?' asked Oosha, who had been doing her best to follow the conversation.

'Snark,' said Iggy. 'He hates us.'

'He's a noggerhead!' muttered Hubba.

Oosha looked puzzled.

'But I not know any Snork. Why he come for?'

'Don't ask me,' said Iggy. 'But it looks like we're stuck with him.'

To tell the truth he was as mystified as they were. In his experience Snark never helped anyone but himself, so why would he volunteer

37

for a dangerous trip to the Cloud Mountains?

*   *   *

In a dark cave further down the hill, Snark was asking the same question.

'Why me?' he complained sulkily. 'Why can't you go?'

'Don't be a dungwit!' snapped his father. 'I'm Chief of the elders—how can I go? I'm far too important.'

'Then let Iggy take her. He wants to,' said Snark. 'And if he dies, no one'll care!'

Borg shook his head. 'Hasn't you been listening, boy? I want *you* to go. They need a good hunter.'

Snark sniffed. It was true he was a brilliant hunter. He was brilliant at a lot of things—boulder-ball, climbing trees, bullying—but hunting came as naturally to him as breathing. Other boys of his age fainted at the sight of blood; he actually *enjoyed* it. All the same, this wasn't a hunting trip or he might have been more enthusiastic. The point was to escort this Henna

38

girl back to her tribe. But the question was—why bother? She could find her own way home, and if she got eaten by wolves then too bad– who was going to know? In any case, he didn't see why he should tramp halfway across the world to find some tribe he'd never even heard of. He tossed the bone he'd been chewing into a corner.

'But what's the point?' he grumbled.

His father slipped a hand inside his furs and drew something out.

'There,' he said. 'There's your point.'

'Huh!' grunted Snark. 'A stone.'

'Take a proper look.'

Snark took the smooth red stone

over to the fire where he could see it better. It was different from any stone he'd seen before. This one shimmered with light, like a fish just before you bashed it on the head.

'Ever seen anything like it?' asked Borg.

'Never.' Snark shook his head. 'Can I keep her?'

'Don't be stupid—give her here.' Borg snatched the stone and held it up. 'Now listen. Say I got twenty of these stones, what then?'

'You need a sack.'

'I got power, you dungwit, that's what. People love these firestones— they'll give anything for 'em. Hammerhead most of all.'

'But he's the Chief,' said Snark. 'If he likes 'em so much, why don't he just get some?'

Borg shook his head. 'That's the beauty of it, boy. They're rare. You only find 'em in the Cloud Mountains, where the Henna live.'

He paused, waiting for Snark to work it out. It took a while.

'Oh! That's why you want me to go!

You want them firestones.'

'Exactly. And not just a few, mind. I want twenty or more.'

'Twenty or more,' repeated Snark. 'You mean like a million?'

Borg sighed. 'Never mind. Get some sleep. You got a long journey tomorrow.'

Snark went to the back of the cave to lie down while Borg remained sitting by the smoky fire, thinking evil thoughts. Once he had the firestones, he would string them into a necklace and invite Hammerhead over to see them. The old fool wouldn't be able to resist the sight of all those sparkling stones. He would give anything in exchange, even the ceremonial necklace that was his prize possession. Once Borg had that it would be easy to persuade those gormless elders that he was the rightful Chief. Borg, High Chief of the Urks. It sounded good.

Chapter 5

Journey to Cloud Mountains

Early next morning Iggy, Hubba and Oosha set off on the long journey to the Cloud Mountains and the Land of the Henna. At the foot of the hill they found Snark waiting for them armed with his spear and long-handled axe.

'Right,' he said. 'We got a long journey, so let's get one thing straight: I'm in charge.'

Iggy and Hubba looked at each other.

'How come?' said Iggy.

''Cos I say so, numlugs. I'm the oldest and I got the brains.'

'Brains of an ant,' muttered Iggy.

'What you say?'

'Nothing.'

'What if we don't want you giving us orders?' asked Hubba.

Snark took a step closer. 'Then I

might have to learn you, Dum-Dum. Got that?'

Hubba glared but said nothing. It was pointless to argue with Snark when he was in this kind of mood. He was bigger and stronger than either of them and it would only end in someone getting hurt—though obviously not Snark.

They walked on, wading across the river and entering the forest. Oosha caught up with Iggy and spoke in a low voice.

'This Snork. I not like him.'

'No, nor me,' agreed Iggy.

'He show-off. Big belly.'

'Big bully,' smiled Iggy. 'But you're right, big belly too.'

'What he want anyways?' Oosha went on crossly. 'Why he come for?'

Iggy watched Snark striding on ahead of them. He had given the question some thought, but he had yet to come up with an answer. Maybe when they reached the Cloud Mountains they would find out. In the meantime he decided to keep a close eye on Snark—he was definitely up to something.

*　　　*　　　*

They walked for four long days, leaving
the forest behind and crossing a dismal
wilderness where the wind howled
like a wolf. They soon lost sight of
the Cloud Mountains but Iggy hoped
that Oosha could find her way. On the
fourth evening, Snark announced they
would make camp in the shelter of a
clump of trees.

'You two find some food,' he
ordered. 'Oosha make a fire.'

'And what are you going to do?'
asked Iggy.

'Keep watch,' said Snark, making
himself comfortable. 'Someone's got
to.'

By the time Iggy and Hubba

returned, Oosha had the fire going while Snark was evidently keeping watch with his eyes closed. Oosha had made one of her tasteless stews in which soggy green bits floated round in circles. Iggy flopped down wearily by the fire.

'We didn't catch any rabbits,' he said. 'We saw a lizard but Hubba frightened it off.'

Oosha nodded, stirring the stew with a stick.

'Oosha not eat rabbit,' she said.

'What do you eat?' asked Hubba.

Oosha looked at him sharply. 'Nut,' she said. 'Leaf.'

'Great,' said Iggy. 'Nut-leaf stew it is.'

'Can't wait,' said Hubba gloomily.

*　　　*　　　*

Later that night Iggy woke up. The fire had died low and it was as cold as the Ice Age. Hubba was talking in his sleep as usual, mumbling something about roast meat, but that wasn't what had disturbed Iggy. He had the uneasy feeling they weren't alone. Pulling his furs around him, he sat up and stared into the darkness. Nothing stirred except the long grass and the trees sighing in the wind.

'Hello?' he called. 'Who's there?'

His voice died away on the wind. Searching around for dry twigs, he tried to rekindle the fire. For a few brief seconds it flared into life and he thought he glimpsed something beyond the tree: a shadow watching them. But when he looked again it was gone. Perhaps it was just his imagination or the darkness playing tricks? He decided if he was going to lie awake feeling scared he might as well have company.

'Hubba!' he whispered, shaking him by the shoulder.

'Noo! It's mine!' moaned Hubba.

'Hubba! Wake up! There's someone out there!'

Hubba rolled on to his back and opened his eyes. 'Uhhh? What? Where?'

'There! I think I saw something.' Iggy pointed to the clump of spindly trees where the shadow had appeared.

'A wolf?' said Hubba, sitting up and feeling around for his spear.

'Maybe not. It was bigger.'

'You probably imagined it,' whispered Hubba.

'Probably.'

They huddled closer together in the darkness, knowing there was no point in trying to get back to sleep.

'Shh! What's that noise?' hissed Hubba.

They listened. A low wheezing came from somewhere close by.

'It's Snark. He snores.'

'Shall us throw a rock?'

Neither of them moved.

'Look!' cried Iggy suddenly.

Beyond the trees, a bright plume of fire lit up the darkness. Seconds later they saw another and another, until everywhere they looked there were torches like red eyes. They formed a rough line, moving closer.

'Iggy,' breathed Hubba, 'I don't think them are wolves.'

Iggy's heart beat faster. It was too late to run and there was nowhere they could hide.

'Better wake the others,' he said. He grabbed his boo and arrow—at least he would get the chance to try it out before he died.

The line of torches was close now and he could see the dark shapes of men holding them. There were far too many to count. Oosha and Snark appeared next to him, looking pale and frightened.

'What do we do now, oh leader?' asked Iggy.

They closed ranks—as much as they could with only four of them. The enemy had them surrounded and Iggy could make out their faces in the flickering torchlight. They were clothed in brown and grey furs but there any resemblance to Urks came to an end. At first Iggy thought they were dark skinned but now he saw they were painted head to foot in what looked like red mud. Their hair was red too and coiled in loops, ponytails, or topknots that bobbed about like hairy pompoms. In their hands they carried short spears carved with magic symbols and the faces of weird beasts. Iggy doubted if they were here to ask directions.

A giant man who appeared to be the tribal Chief stepped forward. His long red hair trailed down his back. Round his neck were strings of shells threaded with brilliant stones that Iggy immediately recognised. Firestones! He drew out an evil-looking dagger and pointed it at Iggy's head.

'BLUDMUGGER!'

'Erm, thanks,' said Iggy. 'But actually we've already eaten.'

Chapter 6

The Big Cheat

The Chief took a step closer. Iggy pulled back the bowstring ready to let go. Suddenly Oosha burst between them and threw her arms round the stranger's neck.

'PAPPA!'

Hubba lowered his spear. 'You think they know each other?'

'Looks that way,' replied Iggy. 'They must be Henna.'

'Thank Urk! Then they're not gonna kill us?'

The men crowded round Oosha, patting her head and jabbering all at once in their own strange language. Eventually, when things had calmed down, she turned to Iggy to explain.

'This my Pappa. Karratop, Big Cheat of Henna.'

Iggy bowed low before the Big Cheat and Hubba did the same. He certainly was big. He made Hammerhead look like a stick insect. Iggy nudged Snark, who was so busy staring at the firestones round the Chief's neck that he'd forgotten to bow.

They waited while Oosha and her father talked. They obviously had a lot to catch up on. At one point the conversation seemed to get heated because the Chief jabbed his finger at them and growled something about Bludmuggers. Finally Oosha came over to explain.

'I tell Pappa you brave worrier. Save Oosha life. He make thank.'

Karratop threw a meaty arm round Iggy's shoulder. 'THANK!' he bellowed. Then he said something to Oosha.

'Pappa say we go now,' she said.

'Go where?' asked Hubba.

'Mountains. Not many walk. Pappa say we want you for suppers.'

Iggy laughed. 'You mean he wants us to *stay* for supper?'

Oosha looked confused. 'Yes, stay—this what he say.'

Iggy could see how the Cloud Mountains got their name. Once they had climbed to the top they were surrounded by a thick grey mist. As they inched their way down the slope towards the Henna camp, the mist cleared and Iggy could see smoke rising from a dozen fires. Instead of caves there was a ring of straw huts, which from above looked like hairy mammoths fast asleep. People went in and out of these huts as if it was the most natural thing in the world.

Their arrival caused quite a stir.

Children came running from all directions. Iggy watched the Henna women greeting their returning menfolk. Like Oosha, the women all had flame-red hair and wore bangles and necklaces made of firestones. Many of them looked as if they could hold their own in a wrestling match. The three young Urks soon caught their attention and the women crowded round, pulling their hair and squeezing their flesh.

'What do they want?' cried Iggy, trying to escape from a woman pinching his leg.

Oosha laughed. 'They never see Urg boy. They say you good looker.'

Snark was attracting the most attention. Two Henna girls had seized him by the arms and were fighting over him in a tug of war. Iggy and Hubba left him to it and went off with Oosha to take a look at the Henna camp.

The huts were arranged in a rough circle. Oosha showed them the largest one which belonged to her father, the Big Chief. Judging from the smell, it was made from a mixture of straw and

53

mammoth dung. It was smaller but less draughty than Iggy's cave, with a hole in the roof to let the smoke from the fire escape. Around the door they found a group of women preparing food for later that evening.

'What is it?' asked Iggy, peering into the pot they were stirring.

'Stew. Very good,' answered Oosha.

'Isn't there any meat?' moaned Hubba, who felt that if he didn't get a proper meal soon he was going to die of hunger.

'We not eat animal,' said Oosha.

'Not ever?' said Hubba. 'Not even lizard?'

Oosha shook her head. 'Why I eat lizard?'

''Cos it tastes good,' said Hubba.

Oosha looked away. 'Many thing taste good,' she said with a sigh. She watched a group of laughing children run by, chasing each other. One of the old women who had been stirring the pot approached Iggy. She was holding something cupped in her hands which turned out to be some kind of drink in a shell.

'*Slorp!*' she said, grinning through gap teeth.

'She say drink. You thirsty,' explained Oosha.

It was true Iggy's throat was parched, but the drink didn't look tempting. It was dark green and reminded him of looking up Hubba's nose—something he tried to avoid.

'What is it?' he asked.

'*Slorp*,' repeated the old woman, pushing the shell into his hands. Iggy felt it would be rude to refuse. He raised the shell to his lips, taking a large mouthful. It tasted even more disgusting than it looked.

'Mmm, good *slorp*,' he said, wiping his lips. He passed the shell to Hubba, who drank some too.

Iggy glanced round. 'What happened to Snark?'

*   *   *

Snark was sitting

in one of the straw huts with the girl who had claimed him as her prize in the tug of war. Her name seemed to be Magg. Magg had a tangle of thick red hair, strong arms and eyebrows that met in the middle. She moved a little closer to Snark—closer than he would have liked.

'Well,' he said, moving away. 'This is cosy. Is this your cave, like?'

Magg leaned towards him. For a horrible moment he thought she was going to kiss him, but instead she sniffed his ear. He shuffled away again, ready to make a break for the door. Like all the Henna, Magg was wearing a necklace with a single large firestone. He pointed to it now.

'That's a pretty necklace.'

'Negless?' said Magg.

'Yes. That's a firestone, isn't it?'

Magg stared at him.

'Where'd you get it? Only I were thinking my grandma would like one.'

'Uhh?'

This obviously wasn't going to get them anywhere. It wasn't easy extracting information from someone whose conversation consisted mainly of 'Uhhhs'.

'Mind if I take a look?' he asked.

'Uhh?'

Very slowly, so as not to startle her, Snark reached out a hand towards the firestone. His fingers closed over it— just before she bit him.

'YEEARGHHHHH!' he howled.

Snark sat for a minute, examining the small teeth marks on the back of his hand. Magg had gone off somewhere— maybe to find someone else to bite. Getting up to go, it dawned on him that there was no one about. He should make a proper search of the hut while he had the chance. It didn't contain much: some skins and furs piled in a corner, an assortment of flint tools and weapons. He looked under the furs and poked among the tools. Nothing. He glanced up at the roof. Where would the Henna hide something valuable?

Five minutes later he was interrupted by a voice.

'What on Urk are you doing?'

Snark whirled round guiltily. Iggy and Hubba were standing in the doorway.

'Nothing!'

Hubba pointed. 'You made a hole in the roof!'

'Oh yeah. I were just looking . . . to see what it's made of. Dung mostly.'

He brushed dirt and bits of straw off his hands.

'Anyway, leave it because we're going,' said Iggy, putting out a hand to steady himself.

'What?'

'Going home—while it's still . . . uhh . . . light.' All of a sudden he wasn't feeling so good. The ground seemed to be sliding away from him.

Snark stared at them. 'We can't go yet!'

'Why not?' said Iggy.

'Because . . . You heard, they want us to stay for supper.'

Hubba wiped his forehead. 'We'll tell 'em we can't. Anyway, it's only nut stew.'

'NO!' shouted Snark, thumping his fist against the wall. 'I'm the leader and I say we stay!'

Iggy sank to his knees. He hadn't

meant to but suddenly his legs felt like jelly and his head was spinning. The faces before him blurred as if they were underwater.

'You stay,' he mumbled. 'Me 'n' Hubble going home.' What was wrong with him? He seemed to be having trouble with his weirds. His head swam as Snark came closer and bent over him.

'Listen,' he whispered. 'Hasn't you seen what they wear? They all got them!'

But Iggy couldn't hear him. He had slumped face down in the dirt. Snark turned to find that Hubba was lying down too, apparently too tired to talk any more. It was very strange. He looked up. An old woman was standing in the doorway, smiling at him through gap teeth.

'*Slorp*,' she said, holding out a shell to him.

Chapter 7

Frying Tonight

Iggy opened his eyes. For a moment he imagined he was back home. Any moment now he would hear his dad muttering curses as he tried to light the fire. But this didn't look like his own cave or smell like it. It smelt wrong. He sat up with an effort. His head throbbed as if someone had been using it to crack walnuts. They were in a damp, gloomy cavern with a high ceiling.

'How you feeling?' asked Hubba, squatting down in front of him.

'Urrgh! Where are we?'

Hubba glanced around. 'Dunno. Some sort of cave.'

'Yes, but I mean how did we get here?'

Iggy tried to remember what had happened. He remembered going into a hut and finding Snark there, pulling bits out of the roof. That was when the dizziness took over and he must have passed out. But why? He'd had nothing to eat apart from . . .

'Of course!' he said. 'The drink!'

'I know,' said Hubba. 'It were disgusting! No wonder we all got sick.'

'They put something in it,' said Iggy, rubbing his head.

He remembered the bitter taste and the way the old woman had been eager for him to taste it. It seemed a funny way to treat honoured guests. He wondered what they were doing in this cave and what their hosts had in mind for them.

'This is all your fault.' Iggy looked up to see Snark standing over him.

'Mine?' he said. 'I thought you were the leader.'

'It weren't my idea to come.'

'Then why did you?' scowled Hubba. 'No one asked you.'

'Shut up, Dum-Dum!'

'You shut up!'

Snark pushed Hubba in the chest so that he staggered backwards. Iggy stood up quickly and came between them.

'For Urk's sake! It's no use fighting,' he said. 'If we're going to get out of here, we've got to stick together.'

Snark and Hubba glared at each other, breathing hard. 'We can't get out,' said Snark flatly.

'Why not?'

'There's guards outside. I been to look.'

So they were prisoners. Iggy looked around. At the far end of the cavern there was a small passageway leading off into darkness.

'What about that way?' he asked. Snark shrugged. It was probably a dead end but there was no harm in looking.

They crept along the passage in single file with Iggy leading the way. In places the roof was so low that they had to bend double. Iggy had the feeling they were tunnelling deeper and deeper under the mountain, but it was so dark he had no way of telling. Snark tugged at his arm.

'Let's go back!'

'What for?'

'It's dark. I don't like it!'

At last the passage began to widen out and they could walk upright without bashing their heads. Iggy could see dim light ahead. Maybe they had found a secret way out? But when they turned the corner they found themselves in a second chamber smaller than the first. It was lit by flaming torches that left black scorch marks on the ceiling. Iggy stared. The walls were criss-crossed with shining red veins and filling the middle of the cave was something even more startling—a dazzling heap of stones, piled almost to the roof.

'Firestones!' gasped Snark.

'There must be twenty!' said Hubba, who wasn't good at big numbers.

Snark went closer. He sank to his knees and scooped up handfuls of stones, letting them run through his fingers like coins. Imagine what his dad would say if he could see this!

Iggy grabbed hold of his arm. 'Snark. Leave them.'

'What?'

Iggy pointed. Buried in the heap was something else, something smooth and dirty-white that made him reluctant to look too close. He bent down and scraped some of the stones aside. It was a skull.

Hubba leapt back as if he'd been bitten. 'Ugh! I thought they don't eat animals.'

'That's not an animal,' said Iggy.

They all stared. Now their eyes had adjusted to the gloom they noticed more skulls—a lot more, cracked and grinning with missing teeth, buried in the heap like grim warning signs.

The hair prickled on Iggy's neck. Something was wrong here, something that had been bothering him since they'd first arrived. Why would the Henna go to so much trouble to prevent them leaving, doctoring their drink and dumping them in this cave? He remembered how the women had greeted them on their arrival, pinching their flesh and smelling them almost as if they were meat.

A cold shiver ran through him. Meat. The Henna didn't hunt animals for their food because they hunted something else. And here was the

proof—human skulls, hundreds of them hidden in a cave. 'We want you for suppers,' Karratop had said. Iggy had taken it as an invitation but it turned out they *were* supper.

'Hubba,' gulped Iggy, 'we've got to get out of here. They're planning to eat us.'

'What?'

'They're cannibals! Look around you!'

Snark didn't seem to be paying attention. He was down on his hands and knees, stuffing handfuls of firestones into his furs.

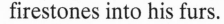

'Leave them!' cried Iggy, grabbing his arm.

Snark shook him off. 'You go. I'll catch you up!' His furs were beginning to bulge as if he'd put on weight.

'There isn't time!' said Iggy.

'Listen!' Hubba held up a hand to silence them. The three of them stood rooted to the spot, straining to hear. From far down the passageway came the muffled sound of footsteps. The Henna were coming.

'Quick!' hissed Iggy. 'Hide!'

They looked around the small, dimly lit chamber. There was only one place to hide and it wasn't going to be pleasant.

Chapter 8

Mud!

Iggy didn't dare breathe—not that it was easy to breathe when you were buried under a mountain of stones and skulls. He knew that if he twitched or moved a muscle he would start a landslide and give them away. The footsteps came closer then halted. Peeping out, he glimpsed a pair of dirty, reddish feet. For a Henna warrior they were remarkably small and not in the least hairy.

'Iggy? You there?' called a nervous voice he recognised immediately.

'Oosha?'

Iggy's head emerged from the pile, followed by his neck and shoulders. A moment later Hubba and Snark surfaced too, panting for breath. They crawled out of the heap.

'What are you doing here?' said Iggy.

Oosha glanced behind, worried that she might have been followed. She set down the sack she was carrying.

'Iggy, you not stay here,' she warned. 'You must hurry!'

'Or they're going to eat us?' said Iggy.

Oosha didn't answer.

'You knew this would happen, didn't you?' said Iggy. 'You brought us here deliberately!'

Oosha shook her head. 'No! I not bring you—you bring *me*. I scare to come back.'

'Scared—why?'

'Because I scare this happen! I cross with Pappa! "Bad Pappa," I say, "you not eat Iggy. He save Oosha life."'

'Did he listen?'

'No, he have big temper. Shout, roar, stump his feets. Say Urgs make good stew!'

Iggy nodded. No wonder Oosha had seemed worried when they talked about returning home. Having a cannibal for a father was enough to make anyone worried. He looked around.

'How much time do we have?'

'You go now,' said Oosha. 'When Shani sleep they come.'

'Shani?'

'God of Sun.'

When the sun slept—that probably meant they had until sunset. Iggy tried to think. There was only one way out of the cave and that was back the way they'd come, but with guards watching the entrance, how could they escape?

Oosha emptied out the contents of the sack on the floor. Luckily she'd remembered to bring Iggy's boo and arrow. Not so luckily it came with a big pile of mud.

'Quick! You hurry,' repeated Oosha.

'You want us to throw mud at them?'

70

'Not throw. Make painty face, like this.' She smeared her face with mud, rubbing it into her cheeks. Iggy understood—it was a disguise! Maybe not a brilliant disguise but the best one they had. If they daubed themselves with red mud, the guards might mistake them for Henna and let them past.

*　　　*　　　*

Ten minutes later they crept along the winding passage towards the cave entrance. Iggy wished the mud had had more time to dry but it was too late to worry about that now. He had his boo and arrows hidden in the sack, hoping that he wouldn't need them.

As they neared the mouth of the cave he could hear the two guards talking in low voices. Outside daylight was fading—sunset couldn't be far off.

'Wait!' said Iggy. 'Oosha, come with us.'

Oosha looked down. She shook her head sadly.

'Why not?'

71

'This my home. I must take care my father.'

'He eats people!' said Iggy.

Oosha sighed. 'Still my father. Maybe he learn? I teach him cook vegetable.'

Iggy tried to imagine Karratop and the Henna sitting down to one of Oosha's nut-leaf stews. It might even happen one day. Hubba was pulling at his arm.

'Iggy! We need to go!'

Oosha put a finger to her lips. 'I go first. Let me do talk. Goodbye, Iggy.' She kissed him lightly on his muddy cheek and was gone. Iggy turned to find the other two sniggering helplessly and glared at them. Hubba had rather overdone the disguise so that he looked like he'd crawled out of a bog. Worse still was Snark, whose furs rattled like a biscuit tin every time he moved. There was no time to worry now—Oosha was already speaking to the guards. Iggy and the others followed behind, trying not to look like three muddy Urks intent on escape. Oosha was talking in her own language. Iggy had no idea what she was saying but the guards roared with laughter and turned to look at them.

'*Ulaaga!*' they said, beckoning them forward. Iggy held his breath.

'I tell them you my sisters,' whispered Oosha.

One of the guards was eyeing Hubba. '*Oogla,*' he said to his friend, shaking his head.

'*Ay ay. Oogla boogla,*' agreed the other.

Oosha tapped her head to explain that her sisters were not very bright. The guards laughed again and stepped aside to let them pass.

'We made it,' murmured Hubba as they hurried on by.

'Just keep walking,' said Iggy. 'And don't look back.'

They had gone only a few steps when they heard a horrible sound.

RIPPPPPPPPPPPPPPP!

Iggy's heart sank. He turned round to see Snark looking down in horror. There was a gaping hole in his furs through which dozens of firestones were spilling out.

'Oops!' said Snark.

The guards glared at him and saw the trail of muddy red footprints on the ground.

They raised their spears. *'ATTAGA!'*

Iggy looked at Hubba. There was only one thing to do and it was the thing that Urks did best—they ran.

Chapter 9

Saving Snark

Iggy slowed to a halt and leaned against a tree trunk.

'You think . . . we lost them?' he panted.

'Must have,' said Hubba.

They stood for a minute, bent over and gasping for breath, too exhausted to speak. Hubba hadn't run this fast since the time that girl Uglips tried to kiss him. The angry shouts they'd heard earlier seemed to have died away. With any luck their pursuers had given up the chase. Iggy looked up, struck by a worrying thought.

'Where's Snark? I thought he was with us!'

Iggy put a hand to his head. This was terrible. In the panic of their escape he'd forgotten all about Snark.

'What if they caught him?' he said.

'He can look after hisself,' said

Hubba. 'Anyway, what can we do?'

Iggy met his eyes.

'No,' said Hubba. 'Forget it. Let's go.'

He turned and marched off through the trees in the rough direction of home. After a minute he stopped and looked back. Iggy hadn't moved.

'IGGY!' groaned Hubba.

'We can't just *leave* him!' said Iggy.

'It's Snark!' said Hubba. 'He's a noggerhead! You reckon he'd go back for us?'

Iggy shook his head. 'That's not the point. I still have to try and help him.'

'You're mad! Stark, staring mad. They'll kill you!'

'Maybe,' said Iggy. 'If you don't want to come, just say.'

'I don't want to come,' said Hubba.

'Fine. I'll go by myself.'

'Right. Good luck!'

Hubba sighed deeply. At times like this he wished he'd picked someone else as his best friend—someone who enjoyed, say, collecting birds' eggs.

*　　　*　　　*

76

By the time they reached the Henna camp a fierce red sun was setting in the west. Iggy remembered Oosha had said that the feast would begin when Shani, the Sun god, slept. The two Urks crept down the mountainside and hid behind some rocks where they could watch from a safe distance. The Henna tribe were standing still as statues, their faces turned towards the setting sun. It was as if they were under some kind of spell.

'What they doing?' whispered Hubba.

'Search me,' said Iggy. 'Waiting for something.'

The fire in the middle of the camp had been built up higher, sending smoke and sparks swirling into the sky. Close by sat a large earthen pot, ready to cook. Snark hung upside down, bound by his arms and legs to a wooden pole resting across two uprights. He was stripped to the waist and basted in nut oil to improve his flavour. Even from this distance Iggy could tell he was terrified.

He calculated the odds. They weren't good. Two Urks against one hundred Henna warriors (if you counted the hairier women). If he was lucky, he might pick off one or two with his arrows, but that wouldn't change the outcome.

The sun was setting. A long loud blast on a mammoth horn split the air. It echoed off the mountains and had a startling effect. The Henna fell on their faces as if struck by a thunderbolt, bowing low with their noses in the dust.

'They're worshipping!' said Iggy. 'Come on!'

'Where we going?'

'To rescue Snark!'

They scrambled and slid down the

mountain, stirring up clouds of dust. If any of the Henna had looked round, they would surely have spotted them, but fortunately the tribe seemed to be lost in a trance.

Reaching the edge of the camp, Iggy stole closer to the fire, keeping to the shadows. He prayed that the sun would take its time setting. Reaching Snark, he began to loosen the leather knots tying his wrists.

'No! Please!' whimpered Snark.

'It's me, you fool!' hissed Iggy.

Snark twisted his head round to look at him. Hanging upside down, he looked even uglier than usual. His face had gone bright pink and was running with sweat.

'Where has you been?' he moaned. 'Get me down!'

'I'm trying!' said Iggy. 'They're granny knots!'

He tugged at the leather cords feverishly. The sun was now little more than a thin red blot on the horizon. In a few minutes it would be gone altogether.

'Hurry up!' muttered Hubba.

Snark groaned. 'For Urk's sake! Use your axe!'

'I don't have an axe!' snapped Iggy.

At last he had one of the knots undone—but this didn't improve matters much. Snark swung by his feet, cracking his head on the ground.

'OWW!'

'Shut up! They'll hear!'

'IGGY!' moaned Hubba, his voice rising in panic.

'I'm trying!'

'No, Iggy . . . LOOK!'

Iggy glanced up, sensing something was wrong. The air had turned colder and a terrible silence had fallen. The Henna were no longer bowed in the dust, they were eyeing them like hungry wolves that have just spotted two rabbits hopping into view. Chief Karratop took a step towards the fire and pulled a dagger from his belt.

Iggy glanced at Hubba. 'Do something!' he whispered.

'Me?'

'Yes! Distract them any way you can. I've got a plan.'

Hubba swallowed—his mind was

a blank. The Henna were closing in slowly, certain that this time their enemies had nowhere to run. There was only one thing he could do. Hubba looked down and found three small rocks in the dust.

'Hey! Watch this!' he cried.

He tossed one rock high into the air, followed by a second and a third. The rocks flew round, higher and higher in a blur of speed.

'OOOOOOOH!' gasped the Henna. They had never seen juggling before.

Beads of sweat ran down Hubba's face. He'd never performed in front of an audience, and certainly not one that wanted to eat him. He tried not to think about what Iggy was doing by the fire or what would happen if he dropped the rocks. All he had to do was concentrate and . . .

DUNK!

A rock hit him on the head and bounced off. He lost his rhythm and fumbled the other two. The spell was broken. The Henna growled— this wasn't magic after all, it was just someone throwing rocks about. They surged forward. Hubba looked round, hoping that Iggy's brilliant plan was ready. Snark was on his feet. Iggy stepped into the firelight armed with his boo. He had a single arrow fitted to the string—curiously the pointed end seemed to be on fire.

Chapter 10

Smooka!

Iggy knew that he only had one chance—if he missed, they were all dead meat. The Henna were swarming towards them howling like beasts. Iggy drew back the bowstring, took careful aim and let go . . .

FTAAAANNNGGGGG!

The flaming arrow fizzed like a rocket through the air, soaring high over everyone's heads.

Snark groaned. 'You missed, you idiot!'

But Iggy watched the arrow and saw it bury itself in the roof of the largest straw hut—the one belonging to Karratop. Within seconds the flames caught and began to spread, licking hungrily at the roof. Black smoke billowed into the dark sky. The Henna stared wild-eyed in terror. This was powerful magic!

'SMOOKA!' they yelled, pointing to the flames.

As they watched the wind caught a burning spark, carrying it to the roof of the next hut and setting it ablaze. From one flaming arrow, the fire was now threatening to sweep through the whole camp. Panic took over. Men and women ran in all directions, some falling to their knees and calling on Shani to save them. Others tried to put out the fire by throwing spears or sticks, but this only made matters worse. Suddenly the ground shook with a mighty crash. Chief Karratop saw the roof of his hut collapse, reducing it to blackened straw and dung. He muttered a curse. The Urk boy was responsible for this—the one with the tiny shooting spears. Karratop whirled round to look for him. But there was no sign of either Iggy or his two companions. Once again they had done what Urks do best and vanished into the dark.

*   *   *

A mile away at the top of a grassy hill, Iggy looked back. Above the mountains rose thick columns of smoke where the huts continued to burn. It was amazing what one little pointed stick could do.

Hubba shook his head. 'What you call them things again?' he asked.

'Arrows,' replied Iggy.

'Deadly. But how'd you get 'em to burn, like?'

'Nut oil. Snark was covered in it. While you were juggling, I coated one of the arrowheads in oil, then held it in the fire. All I had to do then was hit the target.'

'Clever,' said Hubba, impressed. 'I'd never have thought of that.'

*   *   *

The journey home was long and tiring. They reached the Valley of Urk on the afternoon of the fifth day. For much of the journey Snark said little, perhaps trying to think what he was going to tell his father.

As they crossed the river a horn boomed out, warning the Urks of their approach. Men and women swarmed out of their caves and stood waiting at the top of the hill as Iggy and his friends climbed to meet them.

Once Iggy had been duly hugged and kissed by his seven aunts and fifteen cousins (not counting Umily), Chief Hammerhead came forward.

'Well, young Iggy. Back safe and sound?'

'Yes, Chief.'

Hammerhead rubbed his hands. 'So then. What about that reward, eh?'

'Ah, the reward,' said Iggy, who was hoping he might have forgotten.

'You got the firestones?'

At the mention of firestones the crowd pressed in closer, eager to get a glimpse of the glittering haul of treasure. Iggy glanced at Hubba.

'The thing is, Chief, it wasn't that simple . . .'

'No,' said Hubba. 'Turns out they was all cannonballs! They wanted to eat us!'

'Great Urk!' exclaimed the Chief.

'Yes,' said Iggy. 'If it wasn't for Oosha, we would never have escaped.'

'But you must have got something, surely?'

Iggy shook his head.

While this conversation was going on Snark had been hanging back, trying to avoid his father. But Borg had seen him and dragged him away by the arm.

'Well?' he demanded.

'It were horrible,' said Snark. 'They captured me and tied me up—'

'Yes, yes, never mind that,' snapped Borg. 'Where are they?'

Snark looked blank.

'The firestones, you fool. How many did you get?'

Snark stared at his feet. 'Roughly?'

'Roughly.'

'Well, counting the ones I dropped . . . um . . . none.'

'NONE?' roared Borg, forgetting to keep his voice down. 'You brainless lump!'

'It weren't my fault!' whined Snark. 'I had hundreds but they was too heavy. Look!'

He showed his father the rip in his furs where the firestones had torn a gaping hole. Borg groaned and turned away in disgust. Why couldn't people do the simplest thing? He *needed* those little stones. How else was he going to get his hands on the High Chief's necklace? He put his hand inside his furs and brought out the one firestone he'd kept all this time. Perhaps there was still a way. Glancing over, he saw that Hammerhead seemed to have got over his disappointment. He was examining a long curved stick that Iggy was showing him.

'And you shoot her like this?' he said, drawing back the string and letting go with a twang.

'Yes,' said Iggy. 'Only it fires these arrows.'

'Arrows?'

'You should see 'em. They're

deadly!' enthused Hubba. 'Better 'n any spear!'

'Really?'

It was Borg who had spoken, pushing his way through the crowd. 'You can kill a bear with 'em?'

'I don't see why not,' replied Iggy.

'How?' asked Borg. 'By poking him in the eye?'

The crowd roared with laughter.

'Like I said, it fires arrows,' repeated Iggy, fitting one of the flint-head arrows to the string. He took aim. The Urks in the front row stopped grinning and took a step back.

Borg folded his arms. 'Deadlier than any spear?'

'Yes,' said Iggy. 'Spears are all right, but this is more accurate.'

'Ahh! More accurate!' said Borg with heavy sarcasm.

Iggy scowled. 'I'll prove it if you like.'

Borg smiled—this was just what he had in mind.

'Please, show us,' he said. 'But let's make it interesting. Chief, what do you say to a bet?'

'All right,' said Hammerhead, who

had never been known to refuse a
wager. 'What's the stakes?'

Borg opened his hand to reveal the
large red firestone. Hammerhead's
eyes shone with greed.

'My spear against this boo stick,' said
Borg. 'If I lose, you get my firestone
and if I win, I get—let's see—your
necklace.'

A gasp escaped the crowd.

Hammerhead frowned. 'My necklace? The High Chief's necklace?'

'Why not?'

'I can't bet that.'

'As you like. Then I keep my
firestone.' Borg snapped his hand shut
and turned away.

'Wait!'
cried Hammerhead. He turned aside to Iggy and lowered his voice. 'Does this thing work? Can you beat him?'

Iggy hesitated.

'No contest,' said Hubba confidently.

Hammerhead nodded grimly. 'You better be right.' He turned back to Borg.

'All right, I accept. What's the target?'

Borg looked around. His eyes roved over the trees and rocks on the hillside before settling on something closer at hand.

'I know,' he said. 'What about you?'

'Me?' The blood drained from Hammerhead's face.

'Yes.'

'Isn't that a bit, like, dangerous?'

'Of course not,' said Borg. 'We're not actually trying to hit you. The winner's whoever comes closest. But of course, if you're scared . . .'

Scared? That settled it, Hammerhead wasn't having anyone say he was scared.

*　　　*　　　*

The Urks gathered at the Standing Stone to watch. There was nothing they loved better than a contest of skill, especially one where someone might get hurt. Iggy, on the other hand, was regretting that he'd allowed Borg to talk him into this. So far he'd only practised shooting at trees and straw huts—a human target was a different matter altogether. What if he missed by miles with everyone watching? Even worse, what if he didn't miss at all?

Hammerhead marched off to take up his position fifty paces away. He stood under a tall beech tree, trying not to look nervous. He muttered a prayer to the Spirits of the Ancestors and took a deep breath, hoping it wouldn't be his last.

'Ready!' he shouted, waving an arm.

Borg stepped forward, having chosen to go first. He was going to enjoy this. Of course he couldn't actually *kill* Hammerhead, not in front of the whole tribe, but he could come close enough to make it amusing. Either way, he couldn't lose. When the boy and his stick failed miserably he would win the contest and the Chief's necklace would be his. Only a moron like Hammerhead would have agreed to such a bet.

Borg flexed his throwing arm. A breathless hush had fallen. Snark handed him his favourite hunting spear—the one with the deadly razor-sharp tip. In the crowd, Umily turned away, unable to watch. If her dad got himself killed, she vowed never to speak to him again.

Borg stood very still with the spear balanced in his right hand. He began his run-up, drew back his arm and let fly with a loud grunt.

HNNNNNNNNH!

The spear flew straight and true towards the target. Hammerhead shut his eyes.

THUNK!

Something splattered on his cheek which might have been blood. He opened his eyes. He was still breathing. The spear quivered in the ground, so close to his feet that it had almost trimmed his toenails. He wiped the mud off his face and waved to show he was unharmed. A mighty cheer went up and the crowd chanted the easy-to-remember Urk war cry.

'URK! URK! URK!'

'URK! URK! URK!'

Borg turned to Iggy and smiled.

'Your turn, boy. Let's see you get closer than that.'

Iggy took his boo and selected one of his arrows (the one that was almost straight).

'You sure about this?' asked his dad.

'I'll be fine,' said Iggy.

'It's not you I'm worried about.'

Iggy took a deep breath. It was too late to back out now.

Under the tree, Hammerhead had taken his post again, resisting the urge to run for the nearest cave.

Iggy squinted through one eye and took aim, trying to remember what he'd practised.

Breathe slowly. Keep a steady arm. Try not to think of blood.

He drew the string taut and let it go. The arrow hummed through the air in a perfect arc.

SHOOOOOCK!

'YAARRGHHH!' Hammerhead yelled out, certain that he was dead or wounded or possibly both. The crowd had gone silent. Slowly he opened his eyes. The arrow had missed his left shoulder by a hair's breadth, pinning him to the tree trunk by his furs. With an effort he pulled it out and held it up.

The crowd roared:

'IGGY, IGGY, IGGY!

URK, URK! URK!'

Iggy's cheeks glowed. No one had ever chanted his name before.

'You did it! You winned!' yelled Hubba above the din. Mum and Dad came forward and thumped him on the back. Even Umily hugged him in sheer relief. Through the crowd Iggy caught sight of an ashen-faced Borg, looking as if he'd just witnessed the impossible. Beaten by a boy with a bent stick!

'IGGY!' boomed the Chief, clasping him in a bear hug. 'Amazing! Incredible! Let me see that thing!' He stared at the weapon as if it was a miracle fallen from the sky. Raising it above his head, he addressed the whole tribe.

'Men of Urk! Remember this day! From now on you will all learn to hunt with the boo and arrow!'

Everyone cheered. Everyone apart from Iggy's dad.

'Flaming Urk!' he muttered. 'It were dangerous enough when they was throwing spears!'